THE CITY WE BUILD

WRITTEN BY KATIE WOOLLEY
ILLUSTRATED BY SOPHIE FOSTER

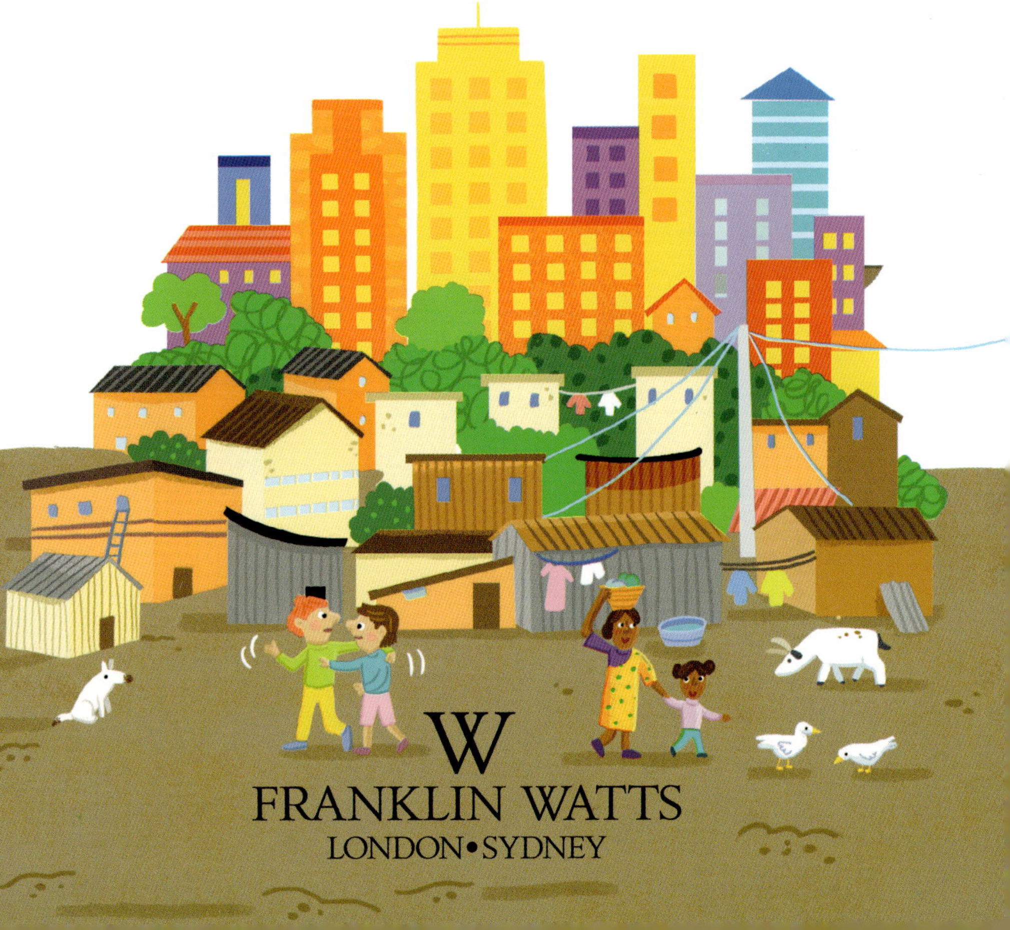

WE GO ECO

W
FRANKLIN WATTS
LONDON • SYDNEY

First published in Great Britain in 2023
by Hodder and Stoughton
Copyright © Hodder and Stoughton, 2023
All rights reserved.

Illustrators: Sophie Foster and Hannah Wood
Designer: Lisa Peacock
Series Editor: Melanie Palmer

HB ISBN 978 1 4451 8267 4
PB ISBN 978 1 4451 8268 1

Printed in China

Picture credits:
Esther Ruth Mbabazi/Reuters/Alamy: 29t.

Every attempt has been made to clear copyright. Should there be any inadvertent omission please apply to the publisher for rectification.

Franklin Watts
An imprint of Hachette Children's Group
Part of Hodder and Stoughton
Carmelite House
50 Victoria Embankment
London EC4Y 0DZ
An Hachette UK Company
www.hachette.co.uk

MIX
Paper from responsible sources
FSC® C104740

CONTENTS

Cities of the World	4
City Life	6
Cities in Trouble	8
City Pollution	10
City Transport	12
City Energy	14
Different Types of Energy	16
Green Cities	18
City Homes	20
A Carbon Footprint	22
A City Community	24
Become an Eco Warrior	26
Earth Activist: Vanessa Nakate	28
Glossary	30
Index	32

CITIES OF THE WORLD

There are cities all around the world.
The first cities were built about 5,500 years ago.

This is Ur, in modern Iraq.
It is one of the oldest cities
in the world.

In the 1700s, cities began to grow.
In the 1800s, in Europe and then the USA,
cities started to change as more and more
factories were built.

People moved from the
countryside to the cities
to look for work.

In the 1900s, cities began to spread out and up.

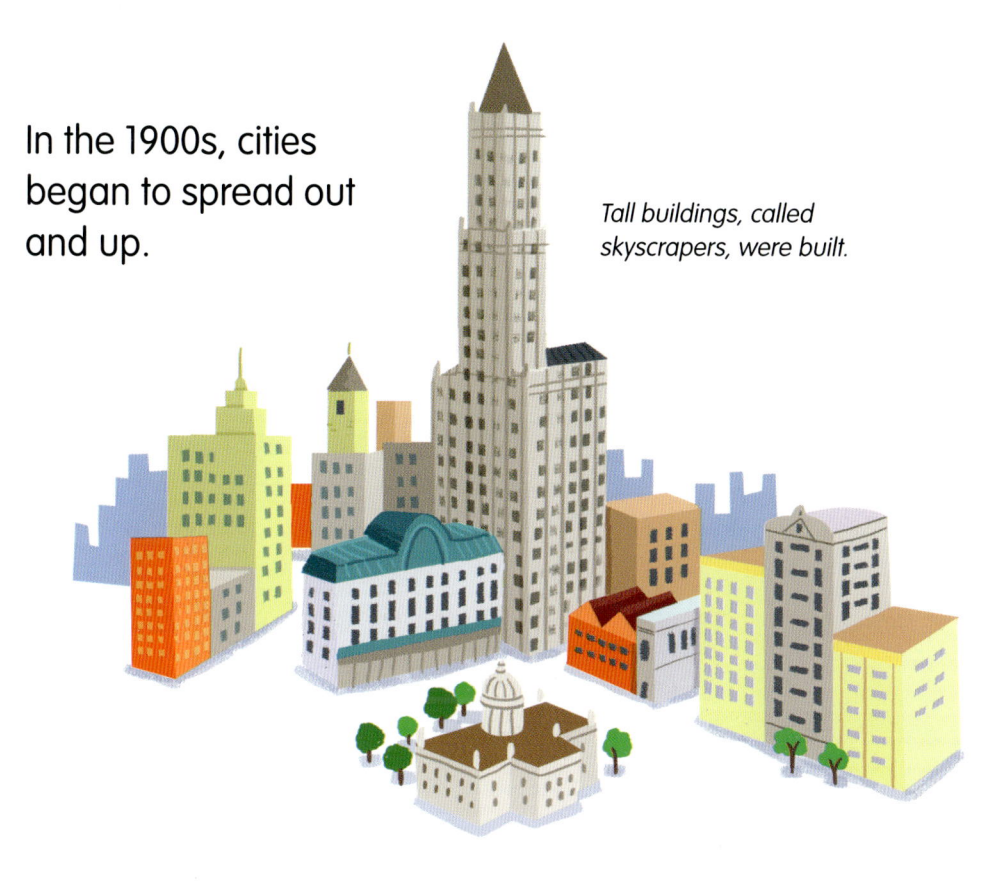

Tall buildings, called skyscrapers, were built.

Today, big cities take up lots of space in countries all over the world.

CITY LIFE

Today, more than half of all the people in the world live in a city. More people now live in a city than in the countryside.

Cities offer people more jobs, schools and activities.

But living in a city is expensive. For rich people, life in a city can be good. For poorer people, living in a city can be hard.

A city is a busy, crowded place.

CITIES IN TROUBLE

Today, cities are in trouble. Earth is slowly getting hotter. This is called climate change. Climate change is causing extreme weather events to happen more often, even in cities.

Floods happen when heavy rain falls for a long period of time and has nowhere to go.

A hurricane is a big storm that starts out at sea but can impact cities on land.

A tornado is a big storm that starts on land, sometimes near a city.

A tsunami is a big wave caused by an earthquake or volcano erupting under the sea. It can destroy coastal towns and cities.

A drought is a lack of rain over a long period of time. Droughts affect cities and the countryside.

A heatwave is a long period of very hot weather. This can cause wildfires that can get close to cities.

ECO-TIP
It's time to 'Go Eco'!

Cities today must cope with more extreme weather every year. But cities are also a part of the problem.

9

CITY POLLUTION

As more cities develop or as a city gets bigger, more buildings are built, more people live there and there are more vehicles on the roads. This means more pollution. Pollution is a big part of climate change.

Pollution is what happens when harmful substances are added to air, water or land.

Smog is a kind of air pollution often found in citties. It is a mix of fog, smoke and harmful gases.

CITY TRANSPORT

Air pollution and harmful gases in the air contribute to climate change. Air pollution in a city can also harm people's health.

Lots of cities must cope with air pollution and harmful gases from busy roads.

People in cities need to reduce air pollution. They can do this by walking, cycling or using public transport instead of driving in their cars.

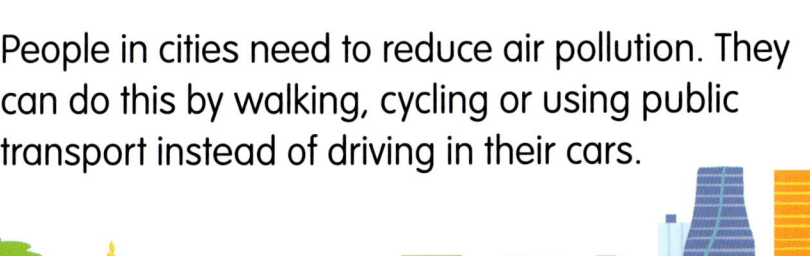

In Hangzhou, China, people in the city hire bikes.

In Copenhagen, Denmark, a bicycle superhighway has made cycling safer.

ECO-TIP
When you are in a city, walk or use public transport.

CITY ENERGY

Cities use most of the world's energy. Energy makes things move and work. Lots of people in lots of cities use lots of energy.

All the vehicles and buildings in a city use a lot of energy.

A lot of the energy used to power a city comes from non-renewable energy sources, such as fossil fuels like coal, oil or gas.

4. Less heat can escape into space.

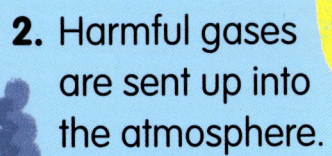

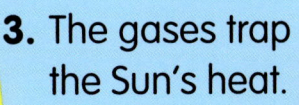

3. The gases trap the Sun's heat.

2. Harmful gases are sent up into the atmosphere.

1. Fossil fuels, such as oil and coal, are burned in factories.

5. Earth gets hotter and hotter. This is called climate change.

DIFFERENT TYPES OF ENERGY

Non-renewable energy sources, such coal and oil, will run out one day. We need to use more renewable energy, such as solar and wind power. It is made from sources found naturally on the planet and does not run out.

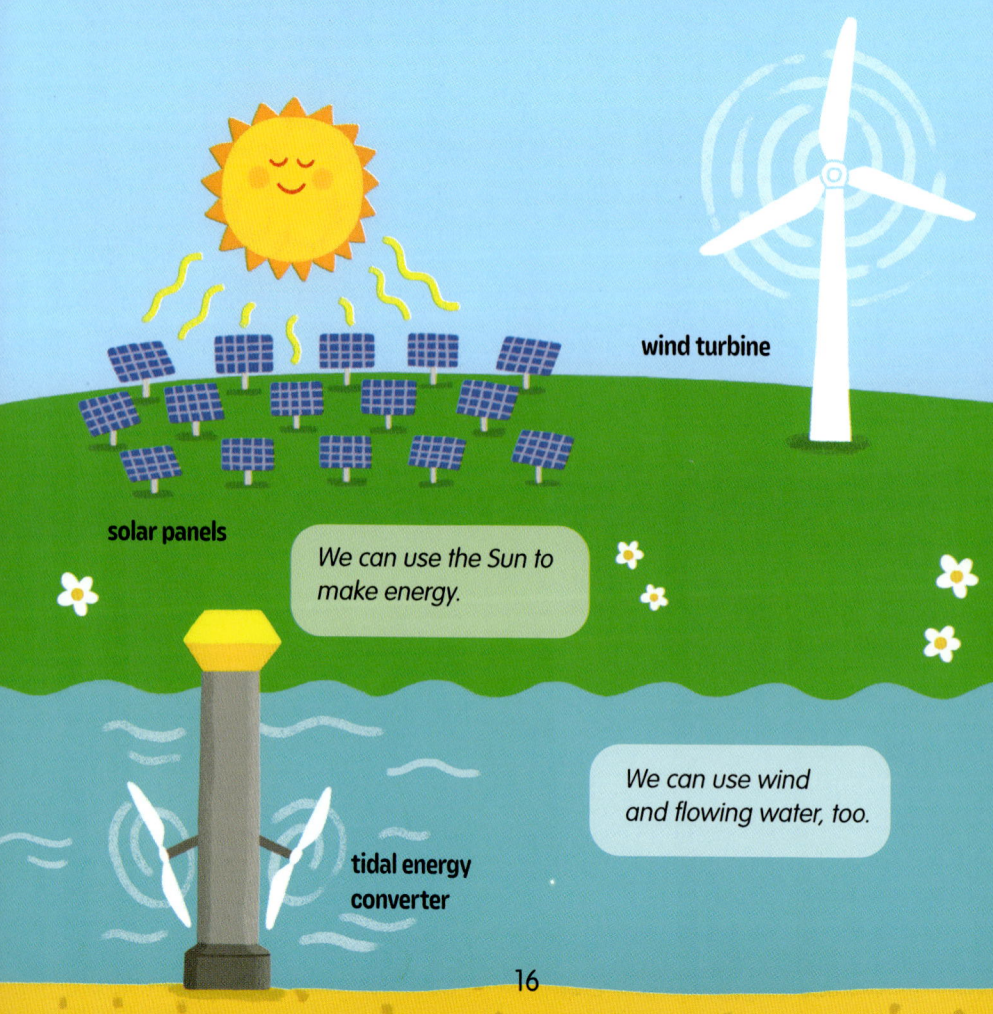

City leaders are looking at ways to use more renewable energy to power public transport, such as buses and trains. Today, there are more electric vehicles on city roads, too.

Shenzhen in China has 16,000 electric buses with 40,000 charging points!

Eco-Tip
Tell your friends all about renewable energy.

GREEN CITIES

The good news is that there are things the people who run cities can do to help save the planet.

They need to look after their green spaces. A park's trees and plants help keep the air clean.

Parks also give people a place to relax outside.

Lots of people in a busy city make a lot of heat. This heat gets trapped, and people often use more energy to cool down. Plants and trees help keep cities cool. They give shade and store less heat than buildings.

Eco-Tip
The temperature in a city can be 3-4°C higher than in nearby countryside.

CITY HOMES

As cities get bigger, we need to build more homes, schools and buildings. Here are some ways we can build new homes and offices that use less energy.

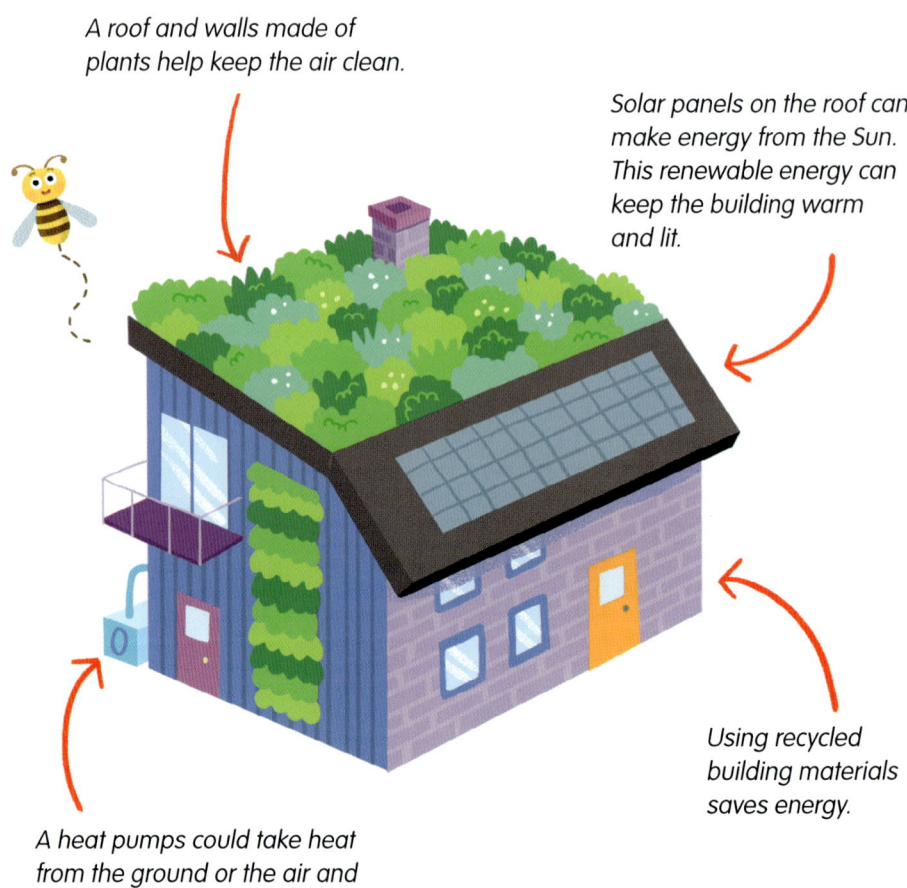

A roof and walls made of plants help keep the air clean.

Solar panels on the roof can make energy from the Sun. This renewable energy can keep the building warm and lit.

Using recycled building materials saves energy.

A heat pumps could take heat from the ground or the air and use it to warm the building.

There are lots of old buildings in a city, too. How can we make them more energy-efficient? One way is to insulate old buildings. This means using special materials to slow down the flow of heat in and out of a building.

Insulation helps keep the building warmer or cooler for longer.

insulation

ECO-TIP
Turn off the light when you are not in your bedroom. This will save energy, too.

A CARBON FOOTPRINT

Every country, city, office, school, home, person and action has a carbon footprint. A carbon footprint is the amount of CO_2 (a greenhouse gas) that is sent up into the air because of energy use.

We can lower a city's carbon footprint by planting trees, walking or cycling more and using less non-renewable energy.

Buildings, transport and the way we live in a city affect its carbon footprint.

ECO-TIP
What can you do to make your carbon footprint smaller?

A CITY COMMUNITY

City communities can find ways to help the planet, too.

In Rosario, Argentina, people can grow food on city land. This creates more green space in the city. The soil used to grow the food can also absorb water – reducing the risk of floods.

People can sell the food they grow at local markets and make money.

In Nairobi, Africa, floodwater often destroys homes. People in the city are working together to rebuild public spaces with strong flood defences.

These public spaces are safe places for everyone to live and work.

BECOME AN ECO-WARRIOR

We can all help look after the planet. The people who run cities are beginning to make changes that will help Earth. But you don't have to live in a city to be a part of the change.

Set up an eco-squad at your school. You could swap ideas about how to make your carbon footprints smaller.

Share car journeys with neighbours and friends in your community.

Grow your own food or help in a community garden. You could donate some of your produce to a food bank that helps people get the food they need.

Arrange a litter-picking afternoon in your road.

Reuse materials to make other things at home.

Pass on your old clothes to other people who can wear them again.

EARTH ACTIVIST: VANESSA NAKATE

Vanessa grew up in Kampala, a large city in Uganda in Africa. Uganda is getting hotter because of climate change. Floods and landslides are harming it. People are losing their homes and their lives.

Vanessa saw this happening in her city. So, she set up *Youth for Future Africa* to speak out about climate change and its impact on Africa.

Vanessa wants us to speak out about climate change, its causes and impacts.

 # GLOSSARY

Carbon footprint the amount of carbon dioxide released into the atmosphere as a result of the activities of a person, business, building or community

Climate change long-term changes in Earth's temperature

Energy-efficient used to describe things that use only as much energy as is needed, without wasting any

Expensive costing a lot of money

Extreme weather powerful weather that is not normal and can harm the planet

Flood defence a system put in place to reduce or stop damage by floodwater

Fossil fuel a fuel made from the remains of old life forms, such as oil, coal and gas

Greenhouse gas one of the gases in Earth's atmosphere that traps heat

Harmful can hurt something

Non-renewable energy an energy source that will run out

Pollution when gases, smoke or other harmful materials are released into the air, water or on to land, causing harm to people, plants and animals

Public transport buses, trains and other forms of transport that are available to people to use for a fee and that run on fixed routes

Renewable energy an energy source that will not run out, such as wind or solar power

INDEX

building materials 20–21

carbon footprint 22–23, 26

climate change 8–13, 15, 28–29

eco warriors 26–29

energy 14–17, 19–22
  non-renewable energy 15–16, 23
  renewable energy 16–17, 20

flooding 8, 24–25, 28

growing food 24

history of cities 4–5

insulation 21

Nakate, Vanessa 28–29

parks 18

plants 18–19, 23–24

pollution 10–13

recycling and reusing 20, 27

transport 10, 12–14, 17, 23, 26

vehicles 10, 12–14, 17, 19, 23, 26

weather events 8–9

32